Obama's Bed

&

A Letter to Kisumu

By

Andrew Maina Kariuki

Dedication

'Obama's Bed' is dedicated to my daughters, and to all the children whose lives were disrupted by the 2007, clashes in Kenya. Many lost their lives or those of their loved ones while others had their families' livelihoods destroyed.

First published in 2018 by
Biqil Publishers
Email; biqilpublishers@gmail.com
Tel; 0722 220 147

Designed and Illustrated by I. Oluoch Otieno
First published in 2018

Email; andrewmaina2010@yahoo.com
P.O. Box 3990, 01002
Thika, Kenya
Tel; 0721 518 616

Printed and bound by
Edgly Brandz Ltd.
P. O. Box 77484
Nairobi.
Tel; 0722810994
Email; info@edglybrandz.co.ke

www.ingramcontent.com/pod-product-compliance
Lightning Source LLC
Chambersburg PA
CBHW070611160726
48003CB00005B/2221

Chapter One

Wanjiku

Wanjiku was a twelve year old girl and a class seven pupil at Kandara Primary School. Her school is located at the foot of Mt. Kenya, two hundred kilometers north of Nairobi. The nearest town from their home is Nanyuki. She was the oldest in a family of five.

She was a tall girl and one of the promising netball players in her school. In fact, she expected to join the school team in the coming year. Her hair was black and soft and she kept it short.

"Short hair is easy to maintain and all it requires is a little oil if you like, and a quick combing for you to be presentable. Anyway, you can grow your hair as long as you like once you are out of this place. Grow it until it touches your heels if you wish! In the meantime, I want it short and tidy," their headmaster used to say while emphasizing the need of keeping the hair short.

Wanjiku fully agreed with him and did not require to be reminded that her hair should be kept short. This was after picking blood-sucking parasites from her younger sister with whom she shared a bed. To remove them, she had to cut her hair.

Lice were not only a major hygiene problem in her school. They were an embarrassment to a girl who was becoming sensitive about her appearance. She could remember her disgust a few weeks ago on finding a louse in her hair. Since she could not cut her hair there and then, she applied a little paraffin mixed with water on her hair which effectively killed them. However, she was left with skin irritation for many days.

Other than the lice that made their home in her hair from time to time, Wanjiku had to fight the other type which infested her clothes. These were of a lighter colour and could go undetected for days. This type was easily eliminated by washing clothes in hot water.

Apart from being a good home for the blood sucking parasites, long hair also required a lot of attention. At least once a week it had to be plaited, taking much of her valuable time. This was not possible for Wanjiku was a busy girl. There was always some task that needed her urgent attention. In an evening, there was homework to be done, water to be drawn from the river, dinner to be cooked and dishes to wash at the end of the day. She was usually too tired at the end of each day to bother with her hair.

Saturdays were not much different even if they did not go to school. There was work to done in the farm, uniforms to wash and of course some more homework to be done. Failure to complete her work had on several occasions earned her a thorough beating from her teachers.

Chapter Two

A Surprise for Class Seven

I have good news for class seven pupils," their head teacher announced in one of their daily morning assemblies.

"What good news could he be having?" Wanjiku whispered to her best friend Ciru.

"Do you know Obama?" The head teacher asked.

"Yes teacher," the whole assembly of over five hundred pupils answered in unison. Their voice was musical.

"Who is he?"

"He is the President of America," the musical answer came in waves.

"You are good pupils who keep up to date with the current affairs."

"Now one more question for class seven pupils. Where was his father born?"

"In K'Ogelo"

"What is the name of his grandmother?"

"Mama Sarah Obama."

"You have answered well. There is an organization known as Mama Sarah Obama Foundation based in Kisumu. Their work involves bringing peace and understanding between different communities. They organize tours to different parts of the country for women groups and schools. I do not want to go into details. Your class teacher will handle that." He was referring to Mr. Kariuki, who

nodded in agreement.

"This organization has chosen our class seven pupils to take part in a tour to Kisumu during the August holiday. The tour is fully paid for and all you will need is a little pocket money," the head teacher concluded.

There was excitement among the pupils as they dispersed to their classes. "Can you believe that Ciru!"

"It's great and I can't wait for the day". They did not have long to wait for the August holidays were just a month away.

"Mami mami, imagine we shall be going on a tour to Kisumu when we close school," with excitement, Wanjiku gave her mother the good news.

"My daughter, how are we going to pay for the tour? Remember we have not completed paying the fees for your sister this term," she was referring to Wanjiku's elder sister whose fees for her first term in high school were in arrears.

"It's not like that mami, some people are paying for our expenses. All what I will need is a little pocket money," she explained.

"Then I am relieved, but Ciku……." this is the pet name they used for her at home, "Who are these people and why would they pay all that money?" Her mother was always suspicious of free things. She believed that nothing came for free. There was always a hidden cost.

"The organization is headed by Mama Sarah Obama, the grandmother of the President of America. They organize such tours between people of different tribes to make them know and understand one another better. She went on to explain that they will be living with host families during part of their stay.

"Will you not be a bother to the people hosting you? Many of you do not eat fish which is like *githeri* in Kisumu." Her mother referred to the fact that fish is widely consumed among the Luos while many Kikuyus eat *githeri* almost on a daily basis (*Githeri* is a mixture of maize and beans boiled together).

"That is exactly why we are going there. We shall learn more about their culture of eating fish and how it is prepared."

"I have no problem with the tour though you still have to inform your father and work at the farm on Saturdays to raise your pocket money." Wanjiku like many other young people in her home area was allowed to work in the flower farm on Saturdays and over the holidays. This was the farm on which her parents worked.

Chapter Three

The Blood Sucking Jiggers

Her father like her mother had no problem with the tour as long as he was not paying for it. "But papa, will you buy me the shoes you promised?" Her old shoes were worn-out and she had been wearing a pair of bathroom slippers when going to church on Sundays. Without much persuasion, her father confirmed that Wanjiku would get her pair of shoes before the tour.

In her home area and many other rural areas in Kenya, many families cannot afford to buy a pair of shoes for their children to wear to school.

Children therefore do not wear shoes to school. Since everybody goes to school barefoot, any student wearing shoes is sneered at. Such a pupil is seen as a 'show off' trying to equate himself with the teachers. After all, teachers are the only people expected to wear shoes to school.

Walking around barefoot was the main reason jiggers infested many pupils in her school. Jiggers are the female fleas which dig and hide under the skin of human beings and some animals. They prefer the soft skin around the fingers and the toe nails where they can live undisturbed. If somebody does not wash his or her body regularly, these flees can make their home on any other part of the body. That is why you find them on knees and elbows of some people.

In some extreme cases, there were pupils who missed their classes because of the wounds inflicted by jiggers. This led the school management to set aside an afternoon on a weekly basis when pupils removed jiggers from one another using pins and thorns. After all the jiggers were removed, a juice from some wild berries was applied into the wounds. It was a painful experience and some of the pupils who had a fear over the pricking had to be pinned down by force.

Jiggers do not affect the young people alone. They also affect the grown-ups. Wanjiku knew many old people in her village who walked with difficulty due to the wounds resulting from jigger infestation.

"To keep away from jiggers, all you need to do is to keep clean. We should wash our bodies regularly and keep our surroundings clean. The floor of your house should be watered and swept daily as well," the Home Science teacher used to advice the pupils.

"Avoid entering the chicken house unnecessarily. Insecticides that kill fleas should be spayed on the floor of the pens where the animals are kept."

Chapter Four

The Journey to Kisumu

On the night before their travel, Wanjiku was restless and could not sleep properly. She woke up in the middle of the night from a dream in which she had been left behind. Well before dawn, she was up and ready to go. Her father escorted her to their school which was some distance from their home.

Despite the chill in the morning, the travelers were excited and looked forward to a day full of fun. The prospect of using a train made the tour even more exciting. By seven o'clock, they were approaching Nyeri, and the clear majestic sight of Mt. Kenya stood high in the sky. The sight of the snow-capped mountain always excited Wanjiku. However, she was not happy because the amount of snow in the mountain was reducing. According to her father, the peaks used to be fully covered with snow a few years ago. If this continued, it was estimated that there would be no snow on its peaks in the next fifteen years.

She had heard over the radio that climatic changes were caused by the cutting down of trees and smoke from factories all over the world. To save the mountain and the environment in general, the existing forests were to be conserved while more trees needed to be planted. This is why her school had a tree nursery which produced seedlings for planting by pupils during the rainy season. So far, they had planted trees in almost every available space in their school and in other public areas. Each pupil also received some seedlings to plant in their homes.

Last year, through the Nobel laureate Wangari Mathai, schools in her area planted thousands of seedlings on the foot of Mt. Kenya. These are areas which had been deforested through illegal logging and the massive fire that had followed.

Due to a heavy traffic jam it took them an hour to enter the city of Nairobi. However, the excited travellers did not notice the passage of the time as they were amazed by the tall buildings and the many motor vehicles on the roads. The number of the people on the streets was also beyond their imagination. They were like safari ants in their ceaseless movement up and down. Like many other pupils in the bus, this was Wanjiku's first visit to Nairobi.

Like a snail, they edged their way to the Nairobi Museum where they were to spend the rest of the day before boarding their train in the evening.

Like any other part of Nairobi, the railway station was crowded. People pushed up and down carrying all sorts of luggage. Wanjiku wondered whether there would be space for all those people. With difficulty, their teacher found their coach and within no time everybody was settled and ready to go.

The ride in a train was another experience for all of them. Its motion was soothing and by the time the sun went down, many of the tired pupils were dozing.

Chapter Five

Kisumu, the Lakeside City

They travelled the whole night through countless stops. By the time they arrived in Kisumu the following morning, the pupils were rested and ready for another exciting day.

Kisumu is not as big as Nairobi though it has its share of tall buildings. Its streets were less congested and its people looked calmer. A representative of Mama Sarah Obama Foundation received them at the railway station. He took them in a bus belonging to Senator Obama Secondary School to a compound in Tom Mboya Estate. This is where the offices of the Mama Sarah Obama Foundation were located. Under a tent, tea and *mandazis* (a type of doughnut) were set and the hungry travelers enjoyed their breakfast.

"Boys and girls, teachers of Kandara Primary School, welcome to Kisumu," Mr. Okello, the manager of the foundation, welcomed them after the breakfast.

"You have not seen the lake but Kisumu is located on the shores of Lake Victoria in Nyanza Province. K'Ogelo, the home of Mama Sarah Obama, who is the head of this Foundation and the grandmother to Barrack Obama, is located some seventy kilometers out of Kisumu on the way to Siaya," Mr. Okello explained.

"By the way, we spoke with Mama Sarah this morning and she asked me to pass her warm welcome. She could not come to receive you personally but you will be meeting her tomorrow."

"Mama Sarah Obama Foundation is the brain child of Mama Sarah. We are involved in uplifting mankind both in and out of Kenya. We do this through bringing peace and harmony between different communities. This year we are devoting our time and resources in working among the Luos, Kikuyus and Kalenjins. These were the communities most affected by the 2007 post-election chaos.

We also have programs for orphans and people living with HIV and AIDS. We

are involved in raising the living standards of the communities we are working with through teaching them better farming methods. We also encourage them to adopt other types of farming like bee keeping, fish and rabbit rearing." Mr. Okello paused.

'During this tour, I believe you will have the opportunity of experiencing the hospitality of the members of the Luo community. You will have two nights to spend with a host family. During this period, there will be no organized activities for your group and you will just be guests in those homes."

"For today and tomorrow we will allow you to enjoy Kisumu and its surrounding areas. You will be sleeping and eating some of your meals at Senator Obama Secondary School. It is the same school which has also allowed us the use of their bus."

The travelers spent the rest of the day sightseeing around the town and took boat rides in the lake. Towards evening, they arrived at Senator Obama Secondary School which is a short distance from Mama Sarah Obama's home.

The school whose buildings looked fairly new is a mixed boarding secondary school. The classes and the offices stood in a semi-circle around the area dominated by a tall flag post. Neat flower beds were scattered around the neat compound. The dining hall and the dormitories were located a distance from the classes and were hidden from view by the tall trees which grew around the school. The boys and the two male teachers were led to boys' dormitory while the girls, together with the two female teachers proceeded to the other one.

They spent the following morning touring the Crying Stones of Kakamega. This is a mighty boulder shaped like a man's torso with a head-shaped smaller boulder resting on its top. It really appears like a man. In the morning when the sun shines towards it, it appears as if tears are dripping from its eyes. For the Luhyas, this stone is of great cultural value and sacrifices are done at this site when the rains fail.

In the afternoon, they visited the *Kit Mikayi* cultural center which like the Crying Stones of Kakamega is another place where mighty rounded-boulders dangerously sit on one another to a height of forty meters. Climbing to the top was exciting and fun to the travellers. It is one of the most important cultural sites for the Luo community and sacrifices and prayers are held under these rocks. It is also a major tourist attraction.

Chapter Six

A Visit to Mama Sarah

The big day and the highlight of their tour was the day they met Mama Sarah Obama. Led by a teacher from Senator Obama Secondary School, the pupils took the short walk in the mid-morning. There was nothing spectacular about K'Ogelo village and the road they were on was like any other in a rural area.

Other than the impressive gate and the chain link fence surrounding the home, there was nothing special in the compound to set it apart from the other homestead they had seen on their way. In fact, some of the homes they had passed-by looked more imposing than Mama Sarah's.

"Is this really the home of U.S. President's grandmother?" Wanjiku doubted.

Any doubt she had ended when they came to the gate manned by two policemen in full uniform. One of them made some calls before the group was allowed into the compound. They were told to wait at a shaded corner by the gate house.

"Welcome to K'Ogelo, the home of Mama Sarah Obama," one of the police officer addressed the waiting visitors.

"We love visitors but I would like to remind you that this is a protected area and all our visitors have to strictly follow the instructions we give," he continued.

"We do not allow weapons into the compound and I believe that none of you is carrying any. Or is there any one carrying a gun?" The policeman jokingly asked. One of their teachers declared that they had carried none apart from pens and a note books.

"The other thing that is not allowed in the compound is photography. No photograph should be taken without permission."

There were several houses scattered around the compound with foot paths leading to the individual courtyards. Here and there, several cows grazed, while

some chickens and turkeys pecked around the compound.

The group was led to chairs which were arranged under a mango tree in front of a semi-permanent house roofed with iron sheets. Its walls were maroon in colour with flowers planted all around it. This was Mama Sarah's house, a very ordinary house and hard to connect with the most powerful man in the world.

Escorted by Mr. Okello, the man who had received them in Kisumu, Mama Sarah approached her visitors. She was a grandmother of ordinary looks and height and wore a long dress with a shawl casually thrown on her shoulders. Like her home there was nothing spectacular about her.

"Hamjambo watoto na walimu (hallo children and teachers)," Mama Sarah greeted the visitors in Kiswahili as she took her chair.

"Hatujambo Nyanya (we are fine granny)," the children answered together.

'Welcome to K'Ogelo"

"Thank you grandmother"

"This is where Obama's father was born and when his time to be with the lord
came, we rested him over there," she was referring to the grave of Obama's
father which was a few meters from the house.

"I know it is strange for you. We Luos bury our dead not far from the house in
which the dead person used to live. In having a grave near, the dead person
cannot be forgotten because we see the grave daily." To many of the visitors,
sitting so near a grave was disturbing. This was because graves are always dug,
out of sight and far from the houses in the area they come from.

While Mama Sarah was speaking, a tray of ripe bananas was passed around
the visitors, "Go ahead and eat. I hope you will enjoy them. They are a product
of this farm."

"I am speaking too much. Is there anyone with a question?" Mama Sarah asked.

Wanjiku hesitantly raised her hand. "Ask my daughter," Mama Sarah encouraged.

"When President Obama visited, where did he sleep?"

"During his last visit, he was a senator not a President. Anyway, he slept in this
very house and you will be shown the bedroom he used. If God grants him an
opportunity to visit us again, I believe he will have no problem in using the same
room."

"How does it feel to be the grandmother of the President of America?" Another
pupil wanted to know.

"I feel proud like any other grandmother with grandsons who are doing well.
However, I thank the Almighty always because my grandson occupies the
strongest seat in the world. It also proves that you people can achieve anything
that you want in this life. The place you were born, your tribe, the colour of your

skin or whether your parents are rich or poor does not matter. All it requires is that you work hard and trust God."

She told them of her times with Obama when he used to visit as a young man. "Obama was a very hard working young man. He used to do all sorts of work in the farm and never complained. In those days, I used to sell some of the things I grew in the neighbouring shopping center. Obama used to carry the heavy load of vegetables to the market for me. In the evening, he would carry home whatever was not sold," the old lady paused.

"What was his favourite food when he was here?" Another boy asked.

"Obama likes *ugali* and fish. He also likes the traditional vegetables," (ugali is a heavy pulp made from maize floor).

In small groups, the visitors were shown the bedroom which Obama had used. It was a small room but held a bed and a stool. There was also a table and a chair by the window. On another wall, a few cloth hangers dangled from nails driven into its surface.

It was a clean room and looked set for Obama's next visit. The visitors toured her farm as well where millet, maize, beans, cassava, sweet potatoes and many other crops grew. There was also a fish pond which supplied fish for her needs and the excess sold to the neighbours.

Chapter Seven

Obama's Bed

That day they took their lunch at the school, together with some class seven pupils from K'Ogelo Primary school. Weeks before their arrival, the guests had been shared out among the pupils. Each boy would be staying with a fellow boy while girls would be hosted by fellow girls. They were to stay with their families for two days and nights.

Wanjiku was paired out with a girl of her age called Adhiambo. She was an orphan and lived with Mama Sarah Obama. Like the other pupils, she picked her belongings and headed to the home of her host. The teachers were hosted by fellow teachers of K'Ogelo Primary school

On their arrival, Wanjiku was received in the sitting room by Mama Sarah who offered a mango as refreshment. As she ate the mango she looked around the room closely. It was a big room with most of its space taken by sofa sets. The arm rests and the back of the sofa sets were covered with table cloths embroidered with beautiful flowers. A coffee table occupied the middle of the room while a cabinet with sliding glass doors, stood by one of the walls.

One door led to the kitchen while another one led to the bedrooms and the bathroom. On the walls, were many old and new photographs of the Obama family.

"Adhiambo, show our guest the room she will be using. Later you two will go to the shopping center and pick a few things we need," Mama Sarah directed.

The room Wanjiku was shown, was the one they had been shown earlier in the day during the visit with the other pupils. She was to sleep in Obama's bed! This was beyond her expectations. "Are you sure this is the room I should be using?" Wanjiku asked doubting that her new friend was directing her to the correct room.

Obama's bed was old and made of finely polished wood with a high head board. It was the bed on which the young Obama had slept on during his visits many

NEW YORK

years ago. It was the same bed he had used during his visit as a Senator. The history of this bed went far behind that. It was the bed that Obama's father used to sleep in as a young man, the bed that belonged to Obama's grandfather as a young man. Earlier in the day, Mama Sarah had told them of how her husband had acquired the bed in Nairobi long before they were married. It was a bed with a long history, a history of men who dared to dream.

"Yes I'm sure. Feel free and enjoy it,"

Later on, she expressed her gratitude to Mama Sarah for being allowed the use of the room. "I thought Adhiambo had made a mistake."

"My daughter, while you sleep on that bed, allow yourself to dream. Dream of what you would like to be in future. Dream about what you will do for your family, village, country and the world at large. Whatever you dream can be realized my daughter. Always remember that the biggest dreamer in our recent past lay and dreamt from that bed."

That night Wanjiku dreamt. She dreamt that President Obama had made an unexpected visit to Mama Sarah late in the night. She had been woken up urgently to give room to the president. This did not bother her and she was even excited at the prospect of not only meeting the president but spending the night under the same roof. This will be one story she would not tire of telling on her return home, Wanjiku continued dreaming.

The president arrived and was received by Mama Sarah who introduced him to those around including Wanjiku. Together with Adhiambo she assisted in carrying his luggage and making him comfortable in his room. Earlier on, they had hurriedly cleaned and replaced its beddings. This dream rolled into another one where she was at the White House to meet President Obama. She was being honoured for her efforts in conserving Mt. Kenya forest.

The morning after her first night as Mama Sarah's guest found Wanjiku refreshed and looking forward for the day ahead. They were to help in the normal household chores like washing utensils and preparing the meals. For Lunch, they were to prepare ugali and some traditional vegetables which they had picked from the farm. In preparing the vegetables, Adhiambo informed her that a little milk had to be added because some of them had a bitter taste.

"We have all these vegetables in our shamba but we treat them like weed," Wanjiku confessed as she enjoyed the meal they had prepared.

"That is the good thing about travelling. You will at least have something new to teach your people," Mama Sarah commented.

Towards evening, one of the workers brought fish for their dinner. Step by step, Wanjiku was shown how to clean and prepare it. That evening, they deep fried the fish and served it in tomato sauce. They took it with ugali made from millet flour. This was the most delicious meal that Wanjiku had ever tasted. She realized that she could make the same kind of dish from the fish that her brothers caught from the river from time to time. They could also easily dig a pond by the river side. This could provide food for the family and the extra cash they were always short of.

That night as she lay in Obama's bed, she dreamt that she had initiated a fish farming project in their farm which was doing very well. She was also co-ordinating the digging of new ponds and the training of the farmers in her village. Their farm was being used as a demonstration farm and people came visiting from far away villages. To take care of the fish ponds and manage the visitors who came for training, her parents no longer worked in the flower farm. They devoted all their time to the farm.

She also dreamt that she had completed her schooling up to the university level and that she now worked with the organization which they had founded with her parents. It had offices in all the provinces and many more were being opened in the neighbouring countries. Their work was to empower farmers in adopting new farming methods while encouraging them to grow the crops which easily did well in their areas. They were working closely with Mama Sarah Obama Foundation and she was a frequent visitor to K'Ogelo.

Wanjiku's two nights as Mama Sarah's guest were over and she was to join the others in the afternoon. There was excitement in their re-union and each pupil had a story to tell of their experience with the host families. This was also their last night in K'Ogelo for they were to take an early morning bus to Nairobi. The arrangement was for them to travel by road so that they see the country-side on their way. A bus had been set aside for their exclusive use.

"When you go back to Nyeri, say hallo to all. Tell them what you have seen and done while here. I believe you have seen for yourself how the people of Nyanza are. They are friendly and love visitors. We are not as bad as some politicians say. We are all Kenyans and we should all live in peace."

"We will be sending pupils from K'Ogelo to your area for an exchange visit soon. I hope they will learn a lot from you as well. Good bye my daughter and come again," Mama Sarah had bid the young girl good bye earlier in the morning.

THE END

A Letter to Kisumu

Chapter One

Escape from Kisumu

Akinyi was my best friend when we lived in Kisumu," Wambui answered her desk mate. She wanted to know the writer of the letter she had just completed reading. The letter read;

Dear Wambui,
It was a sweet surprise to receive a letter from you. I am also relieved in knowing that you have settled down in your new school and town.

My family is fine and they send their greetings. I am doing well in school though things are no longer the way they used to be. Quite a number of pupils and teachers left and we miss every one of you. It is my prayer that you will soon be rejoining us. In fact, quite a number of people have come back. Come back! Life is slowly coming back to normal though it will take time….

Wambui and Akinyi had been classmates for three years at Talents Academy in Kisumu. She had written a letter to her some two weeks ago and had not expected a reply so soon. Both were now twelve years old though Akinyi looked much bigger and older. 'How big is she now?' Wambui asked herself as she remembered her lost friend.

Wambui was currently in class six at Thika Preparatory School. Together with her family, she had escaped in the night from Kisumu during the violence that followed the disputed Presidential elections in 2007.

They left everything behind including her lovely dolls and books. She even forgot to carry her album which contained many photographs of her friends taken on various occasions. Akinyi was one of the common faces in those photographs.

They safely arrived at their rural home in Kandara but after spending more than a week on the road. That was the most dangerous journey she had ever taken and it was only through God's grace that they arrived at all. She cries when she remembers the problems they went through.

Though deep in the night, all the major roads out of Kisumu were blocked with burning tires, stones and even trees. They had used some back streets though the neighbouring villages. At Ahero, the police advised them to turn off and take the road that went through Kisii town. They arrived in Kisii in the morning but the violence had already reached there. They took refuge in the police station where they stayed for the next one week.

During this week, the little money that her father had ran out and they relied on the food that was being distributed by the Red Cross. They had nowhere to stay and they all slept in their car for all this period. It was uncomfortable but at least safe. In fact they were among the lucky ones because very many families were sleeping in the cold.

After spending six uncomfortable nights in Kisii police station, they left early in the morning in a convoy of about fifty vehicles under the escort of the police. They arrived at their grandmother's house in Kandara late in the evening of the same day. Their arrival was a relief to their relatives and the whole village.

"Welcome home my children," her grandmother greeted with tears of joy on her face.

"Thank you *cucu*," Wambui had tearfully responded to her *cucu's*, (grandmother) greetings.

The violence continued in many places for another two weeks after their arrival home and more than a thousand people were killed and many others injured. Many houses and businesses were also looted and burned down.

Through some of their friends who were still in Kisumu her parents tried to save some of their properties in vain. These friends who belonged to the local community were also not safe when going out of their houses. They were also afraid that their assistance to a member of a tribe which was being chased away would turn the mobs against them.

Her parents wept when they received the information that their house had been looted before being razed down. Their hotel business was not spared either. All the furniture and equipment was looted and the building stood empty.

"What I am going to do," her father cried out.

"I am sorry for what happened to you but I will still tell you this. When you left for Kisumu almost twenty years ago you had nothing. You did not even have a wife. Now you have brought home a wife and four children. You should be thankful for this."

"But how will I feed them?"

"Do not worry. God will open a way for you," her grandmother consoled.

Their home in Kisumu had been located a short distance from the road to Kakamega, overlooking the city. They had a breathtaking sight especially in the evening as the sun set. The one acre piece of land had been divided into two parts. The first part was taken up by the house and the garden while the second part was preserved for the animals.

After staying in Kandara for almost a month, they moved to Thika where they rented a house. Their grandmother had sold one of her cows and gave the proceeds to her father. He used the money to enroll all the children into their new school and in opening a small restaurant in Thika town. Life was getting back to normal and everyone was enjoying their new life. However, business was not good as it had been in Kisumu but at least they had a source for income, and something to keep them busy.

Chapter Two

A Letter to Kisumu

A day later Wambui replied;

Dear Akinyi,
I would like to pass my greetings and those of my family to you. They are all fine and healthy. I believe that you are all fine and that you are enjoying your school.

Your letter gave me a happiness I have not enjoyed for a long time. It was as if you were near me like the old times. Let me hope an opportunity will come when I shall see your face again.

Pass my greetings to all. Also include a telephone number through which we can talk in the future. My mum's number is 0721-00……. The best time to call is in the evenings or on Sundays.

Yours loving,
Wambui.

This letter was posted the following day by her father. The reply came in the week that followed.

Dear Wambui,
Thanks for your reply……

Last weekend we went to our rural home and passed by your old home. I could not believe what I saw. There is nothing of what used to be your home. The stones which were left standing after the house was burned down have been looted as well.

Imagine someone stealing stones! The beautiful trees which stood in your home have been cut down and all that remains is a pile of debris at the spot where the house stood. I am sorry to be telling you all these bad news but hope that God

Dear Akinyi

Who could be that evil to burn their property? Wambui stopped reading the letter in the middle and asked herself. What was even more puzzling was the information that even the building stones had been looted.

Who was stealing their building materials? Was it the same people who burned their house? Or was it different people? Who would have the time to steal stones and carry them away one at time? Her finger pointed to some of their old neighbours. This was hard to believe. They had always been so friendly and her parents had actively taken part in the affairs of the village. They attended uncountable burial meetings and their contributions were always appreciated. Could these be the same people who had burned their house and stolen the stones? She was still doubtful.

This piece of information from Kisumu was received with no surprise by her parents. It was as if they knew what had happened all along.

"We agreed as a family that we have forgiven those who wronged us. This includes those who looted and burned our house. It also included those who are stealing the stones", her mother consoled the sad girl.

"But mum that is sometimes almost impossible."

"I know my daughter. But we have to keep trying. Do you remember the troubles that Jesus faced?"

"Yes I do."

"What did they do to Him at the end?"

"They crucified Him."

"Good. And do you know what He said of them? Let me remind you. He said Father forgive them for they know not what they are doing."

"But mum, Jesus is God," Wambui stated.

"That is true. But we are also His children."

Dearest Akinyi,
How are you? I hope you are fine. I was saddened by the news about our home, but my mother tells me that I have to forgive them. It is hard especially when I see the sad look on her face.

There are many times when there is no food in the house. I have also been sent away from school many times because of fees. How do I forgive those who caused all this? I do not know but I pray daily.

The reply came a few weeks later and Wambui could not wait to open it. It read in part:

"I am very sorry to hear about the problems you are facing. I wish that there is something I can do to make your life more comfortable. All I can do is to

remember you in my daily prayers that our Lord may grant your family favour in hearing your prayers.

The school is fine and everybody now looks as if they have settled down. To tell the truth, we as a family had a very rough time during the clashes. It was as if we are not Luos living in Nyanza. There was the general shortage of things in *the market and the shops. The super markets were either looted or closed down. The other major problem was insecurity.*

Looting and theft was no longer done on tribal basis. As far as you had something that was of use to the thugs, you became their target. We could not go to school and stayed locked in the house. Playing outside our house had become a very dangerous thing.

Do you know they even burned our car and that many of the houses destroyed belonged to Luos? It was as bad as that. My dad was saying that we should never have elections because they bring trouble to the common mwananchi…………"

The letter ended with the usual salutation.

Chapter Three

Akinyi Falls Sick

Letter writing had become a hobby that Wambui was enjoying. She had written to her other friends in Kisumu and to her cousins who had moved to America and Canada a few years earlier. Every week she received at least one letter. Of all the people she wrote to, Akinyi was the most responsive and her replies most enjoyable. They gave an insight of how things were in her old town and school.

When a reply to her last letter took long in coming, Wambui became anxious. "What could be happening?" She had no one to answer her question. All she could do was to wait for the reply. A month was gone and no reply had been received. She remembered that she had included her mother's number in one of the replies. Talking to her mother was an easy way of calming her worries.

"May I please use your phone to speak to my friend?"

"Which friend do you want to speak to? I do not have air time to waste."

"*Ai mami.* Is speaking to my friend a waste of your money?"

"Not exactly but talking on the phone costs money and it is expensive. You use a phone on important issues."

"What I want to find out is important," Wambui answered.

"You still haven't told me the friend you would like to speak to."

"It is Akinyi. She has not replied to my letter and it is now over a month. I am worried that something terrible might have happened to her."

"That may not be true. Sometimes, letters get lost. Your letter might have been taken to the wrong place. You might be surprised to see a Mombasa Post Office rubber stamp on it when it finally arrives.

"That is true but something tells me that all is not well with her,"

"I am sorry for that. You may use my phone but do not take too much time," she cautioned as she handed over the phone and went back to the kitchen.

Wambui had written the number on a piece of paper and after a few rings a woman answered. There was no mistake that it was her mother who answered. It took a moment to explain who she was and what she wanted.

"Now I remember your voice. How are you?" Akinyi's mother enquired.

"I am fine but I would like to speak to Akinyi,"

"I am sorry your friend is not here with me. But I will tell her you called."

"Where is she?"

"Akinyi has not been feeling well and she is in hospital. She is being discharged tomorrow."

This was no surprise to Wambui. She had suspected that something was wrong. He friend always replied to her letters without delay. However, she did not expect her to be sick.

"What is she suffering from?" she asked in a trembling voice. Tears were already flooding her eyes.

"It is something to do with the stomach but she is okay now."

"Oh that is bad. Tell her that I will be praying for her. I might also call tomorrow. Wambui concluded hurriedly on hearing the warning tone on the phone. The air time was running out and they would be disconnected at any moment.

Wambui was saying goodbye when her mother came into the room. She was alarmed by the look on her face. "What is wrong?" she enquired.

She told her mother what she had learnt about her friend. Her mother felt sorry and promised to allow her to use her phone again the following day. This was good because she would talk to Akinyi directly.

Things did not work out as everyone thought. Akinyi was not discharged from hospital as hoped. To the surprise of her parents and the doctors, her condition got worse and she was airlifted to Kenyatta National Hospital for specialized treatment. Her mother had wept as she conveyed the sad news to Wambui the following day.

On her part, Wambui could not believe her ears. What could have happened to her friend who had always been so healthy? She wept on many occasions as she thought of the suffering her friend was going through.

"Mum do you think she is going to die?" Wambui expressed her deepest fears.

"Of course not! Many sicknesses are easily treated if detected early enough. Your friend is in the best hospital and will be well soon."

"I do not think I can continue living if she dies."

"Who said she is dying? Your friend will be fine. Trust me."

Though full of confidence, the sick girl was in the hospital for another three weeks. No great improvement could be noted and she was growing weak day by day. She even sounded weak and different on the phone. As much as Wambui wanted to trust the words of her mother, she lived in the fear of the death of her friend.

Chapter Four

Akinyi in Nairobi

Nairobi is not very far from Thika town. In fact there are people who live in Thika and commute to Nairobi daily. Wambui had hoped that her parents would take her to see her friend on the first weekend of her admission. This was not possible because her father was away on some business. By the second weekend she could not bear waiting any more.

It was on a Saturday morning that Wambui in the company of her mother made the journey to Kenyatta Hospital. It had been drizzling the whole morning and it was still cold. The journey was tedious and they had spent a lot of time held up in traffic jams.

A few calls to Akinyi's mother took them to the ward in which she lay. Wambui has a general fear over medicine and things related to hospitals. She rarely agreed to be taken to a doctor unless her illness was serious. Because of this, she could not imagine the possibility of being admitted in a hospital and what her friend was going through.

These fears increased as they passed through the corridors of the hospital with the heavy smell of drugs in the air. It was during the visiting hours and the place was teeming with people. The lifts were the worst with everyone pushing and shoving for space. They were crowded and the smell of the riders mixed badly with the smell of drugs. In fact, at the end of the visit Wambui insisted that they use the stairs.

She was in ward seven on the 5th floor. On either side of the corridor, were many double doors widely open that led to the wards. She could see patients lying on beds or being pushed on wheel chairs. They approached the doors to the ward with unsure steps. The ward was like the others she had seen in passing. However, this ward was for young girls. Many lay or sat on their beds in the company of their friends and relatives. It was hard to find her friend by just looking around. They approached a nurse who sat on her desk and asked.

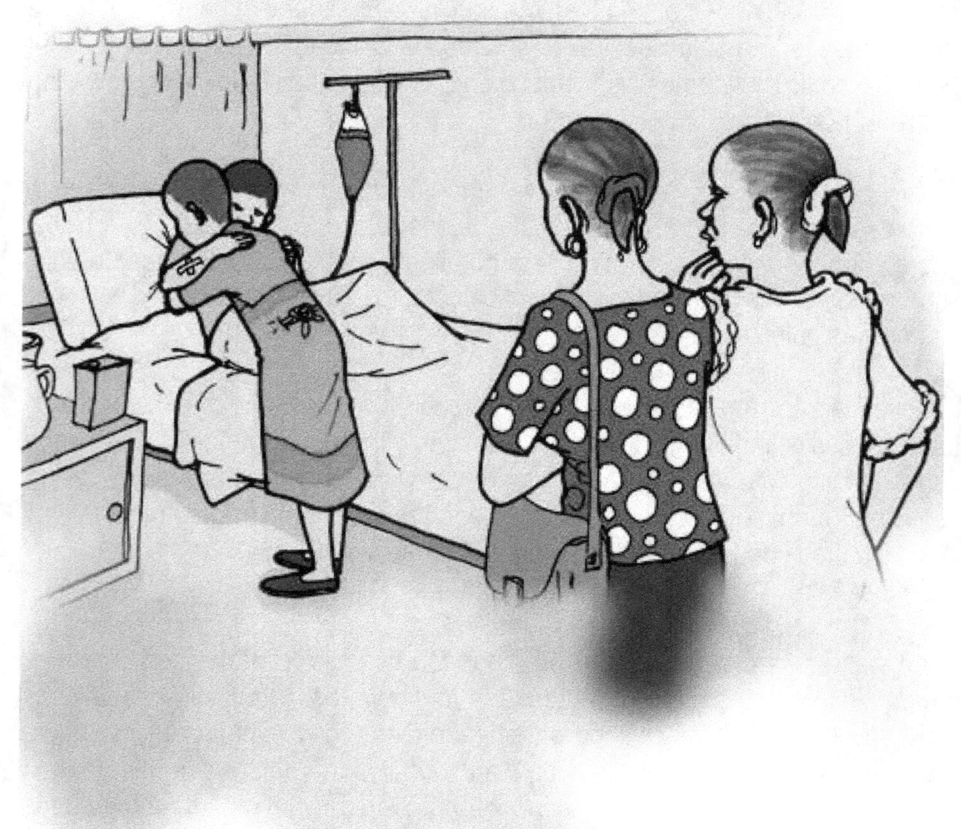

"We are looking for a girl by the name Akinyi."

"She is on the bed next to the second window on that side," the nurse directed.

They moved on as directed but they could have passed her bed. Fortunately, her mother saw them and waved. What followed were long hugs and greetings. Though weak, Akinyi was excited by the surprise visit. Wambui's mother had been worried that the two girls would break down weeping on their re-union. This did not happen. They were too joyful to cry.

"I brought you this," Wambui said as she handed over a small paper bag.

"Wao, these are my favourite. Mum may I have some?" She asked looking inside the small paper bag that contained some samosas. She always enjoyed them. With a nod she allowed her to go ahead. However, she could not eat anything until her visitors had taken one each.

"Mum you have to eat as well. There are still many remaining," she passed the package on.

She now sat on the bed with her feet hanging in the air. She looked thin though she had grown taller since the last time they met. That was almost two years ago. What had not changed was her smile and laughter. Her laugh could still be heard across the big ward from time to time during the visit. Though sick, she could still smile and laugh.

Her mother had changed as well. She looked older and thinner than she used to be. She also looked tired. She had suffered a lot in the last two months or so since Akinyi started ailing.

Though not as close as their two daughters, the two mothers had been forced to socialize on many occasions. They had visited each other's houses during birthday parties and of course met almost daily as they dropped or picked their daughters from school. On this visit, they had a lot of things to talk about as their daughters took a walk to the candy shop.

They talked of the happy old days before the clashes. They also talked of things which had happened since then.

"All these problems have been brought by our politicians. They preach hatred among the tribes then hide in Nairobi when the country is burning."

"It is true mama Akinyi. There is nothing wrong with you being a Luo or of me being a Kikuyu. We are all Kenyans and should love one another."

"It is true. But politicians will win if we allow our children to hate one another. I have learnt a lot from the friendship between our girls. Their friendship is not based on tribe or colour."

Across the corridor and leaning on the balcony, the two girls chatted. There was too much to talk about. They talked about their schools, friends and the many activities they had been involved in.

"How is Thika?" Akinyi enquired.

"It is fine but not as exciting like Kisumu."

"I have been asking my mum to allow me to stay with you. I will be coming for some treatment every week for the next four weeks and it will not be possible to travel to Kisumu every week. By the way my aunt who used to live in Thika moved after the clashes." Akinyi had told her of a visit to an aunt who worked in one of the factories in Thika

"Where did she move to?"

"Siaya"

"Why did she move?"

"She was retrenched last year and she had set up some business in town. During the clashes, she felt insecure and decided to sell the business and open the same kind of business in Siaya,"

"But there was no violence in Thika,"

"That may be so but the tension was too much"

"Don't worry over where to stay. We would love to stay with you. Let's go and ask your mum if it is ok." The two girls approached the two women and made their requests.

"Please mum, can she stay with us for the period?"

"That depends on what her mum would like. When is she likely to be discharged?" she asked, turning to Akinyi's mother.

"I do not know exactly but it will be in a few days' time. She shall be coming back for the clinic every week. I am currently staying with my cousin in Kibera but her place is too small. We have been thinking of alternative accommodation."

"You do not need to worry over that. Come and stay in our place. It is not very big but we at least have a bedroom that the girls can share."

"Thank you Mama Wambui. You are so kind to us. We can stay with you for the period. My only worry is that we might be too much of a burden for you."

"Do not say that again. We can do anything for Akinyi. She is my daughter as well.

The visiting hours were coming to an end and the two girls parted. They were to be rejoined in the next few days.

Chapter Five

Discharge from Hospital

Akinyi was discharged as hoped. As agreed, Wambui's mother picked them from the hospital. By the time Wambui came back from school, the guests were already home. An extra mattress had been placed in one corner of her spacious bedroom.

Akinyi and her mother settled in their new home very easily. Her mother helped in the kitchen or did any other work in the house if necessary. On her part, Akinyi rested most of the day. She also spent time revising using the books left behind by Wambui. They also did her homework together in the evening.

She was recovering well and one could not tell that she had been in hospital for such a long time. She attended all the clinics and at the end the doctor declared that she was completely healed.

Akinyi and her mother returned to Kisumu soon after attending her last clinic. She resumed her schooling though she was still not very strong. As she told her friends of her experiences, she proudly told of the kindness of Wambui's family and of her good times in their home.

During the stay, the two girls had been taken to see the famous Fourteen Falls which is in Athi River. The site was amazing though the water was dirty and had an awful smell as it boomed down the cliff. On the sides of the river, plastic bags old sandals, shoes, clothes and other waste spoiled an otherwise beautiful scene.

"Where is all the rubbish coming from?"

"From Nairobi", Wambui's father had answered.

"Nairobi?" The two girls echoed in surprise.

"Yes, this is a part of the filthy Nairobi river," he answered waving at the river.

"That is terrible. Can't the City Council clean it?"

"I think they do but there is still a lot of pollution as it passes through Mathare Valley and other such places. In some of these slums, there is no sewerage and all the dirty water from the homes is directed to the river. People have to be taught of the need to take care of our environment."

The letter writing resumed immediately. Almost in a weekly basis, the girls exchanged letters. This is what Akinyi wrote after her arrival in Kisumu.

"Dear Wambui,

…Our journey back was safe and nice. I am now in school though there is so much work for me to catch up with the rest of the class.

With all my heart, I would like to say a very very very big THANK YOU for the kindness you showed us. I do not know what I can do to repay you but may the Lord bless you.

I enjoyed my time with you and only wish that you could come and visit us in the future. My mother has suggested that I invite you.

Pass my love to the rest of the family. I miss them a lot and hope to see them soon.

Yours loving,
Akinyi"

THE END